CW00853174

Ladybird books are widely available, but in case of
difficulty may be ordered by post or telephone from:

Ladybird Books – Cash Sales Department
Littlegate Road Paignton Devon TQ3 3BE
Telephone 01803 554761

A catalogue record for this book is available
from the British Library

Published by Ladybird Books Ltd Loughborough Leicestershire UK
LADYBIRD and the device of a Ladybird are trademarks of Ladybird Books Ltd

Britt Allcroft's Magic Adventures of Mumfie
Created by Britt Allcroft from the works of Katharine Tozer
Written by Britt Allcroft and John Kane
Song lyrics by John Kane

Britt Allcroft's
Magic Adventures of

Mumfie™

The Queen of Night

Ladybird

The story so far…

Mumfie, the special little elephant, had set off to find an adventure.

Mumfie met Scarecrow and Pinkey and had promised to find Pinkey's mother.

With the help of a friendly whale, the friends had reached Pinkey's mysterious and magical island, which was ruled by the wicked Secretary of Night.

The Secretary had turned the island into a prison. He had trapped Pinkey's mother along with everyone else — only a mysterious black cat seemed to have kept her freedom.

Mumfie had become separated from his friends and was shut in a room by Bristle, the prison guard.

The room was filled with the Secretary's strange collection of bottles containing birds' singing, bees' humming and children's laughter.

Now Scarecrow and Pinkey had to search for Mumfie as well as for Pinkey's mother...

Mumfie was dusting the bottles in the room when the wicked Secretary's dark shadow fell across the window. The Secretary stared at Mumfie for a moment, then swished away into the sky.

Mumfie watched and shivered.

Suddenly, Mumfie heard a coughing noise. It was coming from beneath a cloth in a corner of the room. Mumfie pulled the cloth off...

Underneath was a raven, sitting in a cage, wearing a medal with a picture of a beautiful lady on it.

"Who's this?" whispered Mumfie.

"This," said the raven, "is the Queen of Night. She looked after all the island from sunset until sunrise." Then the raven explained how the Queen's wicked Secretary had taken over and stolen her magic.

"This used to be the Queen's room," sighed the raven, coughing sadly. "A happy room."

"I can tell," replied Mumfie, "just by looking at the sunshine that's left over."

By now, the dust was tickling Mumfie's trunk. Suddenly, he sneezed. A bottle crashed and golden liquid spilled onto the floor.

The raven pointed to another bottle. "Quick! Sprinkle that grey powder over the liquid."

To Mumfie's astonishment, the liquid and the powder together transformed into a sparkling jewel.

"Oh, how *beautiful*," murmured Mumfie.

"It's the Queen's jewel and *very* precious," gasped the raven. "Put it in your pocket and *never* lose it. It's a treasure beyond price!"

Having tucked the jewel safely away in his pocket, Mumfie asked the raven if he would help rescue Pinkey's mother.

"I can't help anyone," sighed the raven. "I'm a has-been, a failure, a write-off. I couldn't even help the Queen of Night. I'm a waste of your time."

"You're *not* a waste of my time at all," said Mumfie, firmly. "I'm trying to free Pinkey's mother and I'm sure you can help me find a way into her horrid cell."

"You really think I could get my courage back?" wondered the raven.

Mumfie nodded. "Oh, yes," he encouraged.

"Very well, then," decided the raven. "I'm Napoleon Jones, Aide to Her Majesty, the Queen of Night."

"And I'm Mumfie — come on!" said the little elephant.

Mumfie led the way back to the dark, damp cell where Pinkey's mother was trapped.

In an effort to get inside, Napoleon began to pick at the hinges of the great iron door.

Suddenly, a loud whistle startled them – it was Bristle!

"Gotcha!" Bristle cried. "You've broken rule number 439b – interfering with prison property. The Secretary of Night shall decide your punishment. Follow me!"

Mumfie didn't like the idea of meeting the Secretary but with his new friend, Napoleon, for company, he felt a little less afraid.

Meanwhile, back in the room full of bottles, the wicked Secretary was talking to the strange, black cat.

"When I have the Queen's jewel, my power will be complete," the Secretary hissed. "Is everything ready?"

"Nearly," replied the cat. "The potion is brewed and the powder is ground. All that remains is to mix them."

The Secretary looked round the room for the potion and the powder. They were gone!

"The little elephant was in this room," he snarled. "The little elephant has taken the formula!" The quill pen the Secretary was holding grew larger and larger, until the Secretary could sit upon it. Then, as the night wind howled, he set off through the sky to search the island for Mumfie.

By now, Mumfie, Napoleon and Bristle had arrived at the edge of a great floor of ice in the Queen of Night's palace. Bristle rummaged about in a nearby box and handed them some skates.

"Wouldn't you prefer to fly?" Mumfie asked Napoleon.

"Hah!" sneered Bristle. "The Secretary clipped that old bird's wings long ago. His flying days are over."

While Bristle was putting on his own skates, Mumfie secretly scribbled a note to Scarecrow and Pinkey:

SKATES IN THE BOX SEAT,
FOLLOW TRACKS ON ICE.

Then Mumfie stepped onto the ice floor and carefully began to skate.

In their search for Mumfie, Scarecrow and Pinkey had come to a lovely garden. Suddenly, a beautiful lady stepped out of the shadows.

"I am Her Majesty, the Queen of Night," she said, kindly.

"You look very sad, Your Majesty," replied Scarecrow.

"My Secretary wishes to turn all that is good to evil," explained the Queen. "He has stolen my magic cloak of dreams and has used it to imprison all who live here."

"What does the cloak look like?" asked Scarecrow.

"It is big enough to cover the world and small enough to fit into a thimble," replied the Queen.

"I give you my word, Your Majesty," promised Scarecrow, "as soon as we find Mumfie and Pinkey's mother, our next task will be to recover your cloak."

Suddenly, the Queen vanished, but not before the black cat mysteriously appeared. With a swish of her tail she drew Pinkey's attention to the Queen's umbrella.

"Wait, Your Majesty!" called Pinkey. "You've forgotten your umbrella!" But it was too late! The Queen had gone! The umbrella twinkled magically with stars.

Having tucked the umbrella safely under his arm, Scarecrow set off with Pinkey once again to look for Mumfie.

Eventually, they came to the Queen's palace. Scarecrow spotted Mumfie's message, opened the box of skates and quickly put two on. Then, with Pinkey flying, the two friends began to follow the tracks Mumfie, Napoleon and Bristle had left on the ice.

To Scarecrow's surprise he found that he could skate quite easily. *If it wasn't for Mumfie,* he thought, *I'd still be stuck in a field. Life can bring the most wonderful surprises.*

Soon, he and Pinkey caught up with the others. In the commotion that followed, Bristle tripped over his own skates and knocked himself out.

"Out like a light with the bulb gone," confirmed Napoleon.

Mumfie was very happy to see his friends again and introduced them to Napoleon. They all sat down to decide how they could best help the Queen and safeguard her jewel.

Mumfie suggested that the safest place to keep the Queen's jewel would be inside Whale.

So, Pinkey flew ahead to tell Whale that Mumfie and Scarecrow were on their way, and Napoleon set off in the opposite direction to tell Pinkey's mother the plan.

Mumfie and Scarecrow, left all alone, decided to put up the Queen's umbrella. "It will be easier to think in the dark," said Mumfie, as he and Scarecrow sat beneath it.

Suddenly, a gust of wind swept Mumfie and Scarecrow up into the air—they were flying!

"This is magic," laughed Mumfie, as he and Scarecrow rose higher and higher into the sky until the island and the ocean were far below them.

In the distance, they spotted Whale and Pinkey. "Let's wave!" cried Mumfie, taking his handkerchief from his pocket—the very same pocket where he had put the Queen's jewel. This was a bad mistake!

Mumfie watched in disbelief as the Queen's jewel fell away from him and disappeared into the depths of the ocean.

"Oh, no!" cried Mumfie, as he and Scarecrow came down to land on Whale's back.

"How splendid to see you again," boomed Whale.

"It isn't splendid at all," said Mumfie, miserably. "I've lost the Queen's jewel. It's fallen into the sea. We'll *never* find it!"

But Whale said he thought he knew someone who could help them. "You'll have to *find* him first though," he said. "Come inside and meet a friend of mine. She'll tell you all about him."

Inside Whale, the friends met a lady called Mrs Admiral. She told them she lived with her husband, the Admiral, in a little cottage on the bottom of the ocean.

"It's so much quieter down there," she said to Mumfie, "except for those pesky pirates."

Then, Mrs Admiral explained how she thought that the pirates had captured her husband.

"Maybe the pirates have captured the Queen's jewel too!" exclaimed Mumfie.

"Wouldn't put it past them," agreed Mrs Admiral. "Anything is possible with them pirates!"

At that very moment there was a big—
BUMP! The cabin turned topsy-turvy!

"Sorry about that!" called Whale. "Pirates
on the port bow."

Mumfie ran to a porthole and saw a
cannonball hurtling towards them. The pirate
ship was chasing Whale!

"That's Davy Jones' ship," said Mrs Admiral.

"Hang on!" boomed Whale, and
immediately dived below the waves.

Whale went deeper and deeper. Soon he whispered, "We're near your home, Mrs Admiral. Best jump ship while I lead the pirates a merry dance."

"I'll keep Whale company," said Pinkey, who preferred not to get her wings wet!

Mumfie, Scarecrow and Mrs Admiral climbed out onto Whale's back.

All of a sudden, Whale accidentally flapped his tail. Clouds of mud swirled up from the seabed. Mumfie, Scarecrow and Mrs Admiral were sent spinning off in different directions through the muddy darkness of the ocean.

Scarecrow floated the furthest away. He found he was all alone in front of a mysterious lighthouse. He knocked on the door and the lighthouse keeper opened it.

"I'm sorry to disturb you," said Scarecrow, "but I'm looking for my friend Mumfie."

"And what's a Mumf when it's at home?" asked the keeper.

"It's an elephant," continued Scarecrow, "only very little, stands on two legs and wears a pink jacket."

"A jacket like this one?" the keeper said, as he pulled Mumfie's jacket from his pocket. "My good friend, the shark, gave it to me."

"Oh, no!" gasped Scarecrow. "You don't think the shark could have…"

"…Eaten your friend Mumf—more than likely," replied the keeper.

Scarecrow felt tears stinging his eyes but decided to hope for the best and carry on with his search.

Eventually, he found a strange little house made out of an upturned boat. After he had rung the door bell, the door opened and there stood – Mrs Admiral!

"Thank Neptune you're safe!" she cried.

"I may be safe," said Scarecrow, "but Mumfie isn't. I think he's been eaten by a shark!"

To Scarecrow's astonishment, Mrs Admiral burst out laughing.

"How can you laugh?' asked Scarecrow. Then, sitting at Mrs Admiral's table, he saw – Mumfie!

Mumfie and Scarecrow hugged each other.

Later, the two friends snuggled down to sleep.

"This is a real adventure for me," sighed Scarecrow.

"Being under water?" asked Mumfie.

"No – sleeping in a real bed," replied Scarecrow. "I've only ever slept in a hammock in Whale. And before that, I slept standing up in the middle of a field!"

"We must find Whale tomorrow," whispered Mumfie, "and the Queen's jewel, and maybe even the Admiral."

The very next moment, both he and Scarecrow were fast asleep.

As Mumfie and Scarecrow sleep peacefully, little do they know the surprises that tomorrow's adventure has in store for them…

You pull back the covers
And climb aboard bed.
You will glide on
An ocean of sleep.
Your dreams lead you on
While the night winds sigh
Like a lullaby
Until dawn.

But tomorrow will have to wait until the next time!

Book three: **Pirate's Ahoy!**